Tin... a coin

An imprint of Om Books International

Reprinted in 2015

An imprint of Om Books International

Corporate & Editorial Office
A 12, Sector 64, Noida 201 301
Uttar Pradesh, India
Phone: +91 120 477 4100
Email: editorial@ombooks.com
Website: www.ombooksinternational.com

Sales Office
107, Darya Ganj, New Delhi 110 002, India
Phone: +91 11 4000 9000, 2326 3363, 2326 5303
Fax: +91 11 2327 8091
Email: sales@ombooks.com
Website: www.ombooks.com

Content by Sonia Emm

ISBN : 978-93-84119-51-5

Printed in India

10 9 8 7 6 5 4 3 2

Tina finds a coin

Paste your
photograph here

My name is

_____

Tina is five years old.
She is a happy girl.

Tina loves to go for walks.
She takes her dog Choco
with her.

One evening, Tina takes a walk in the park.
She finds a shiny coin.

Before going to bed, Tina
puts it in a box. She shakes
it like a rattle!

The next day, Tina puts
the coin on a paper.

She draws the Sun and
a ball with it!

At night, Tina throws the coin in a jug of water.

She sees the coin sink!

The next day, Tina shows the coin to her school friends. "Wow!" they say!

In the evening, Tina takes
the coin to the park.
She rolls it down the slide!

At night, Tina holds
the coin. She sleeps with
a smile.

Tina dreams that the coin is the Moon.

It shines in the dark sky.

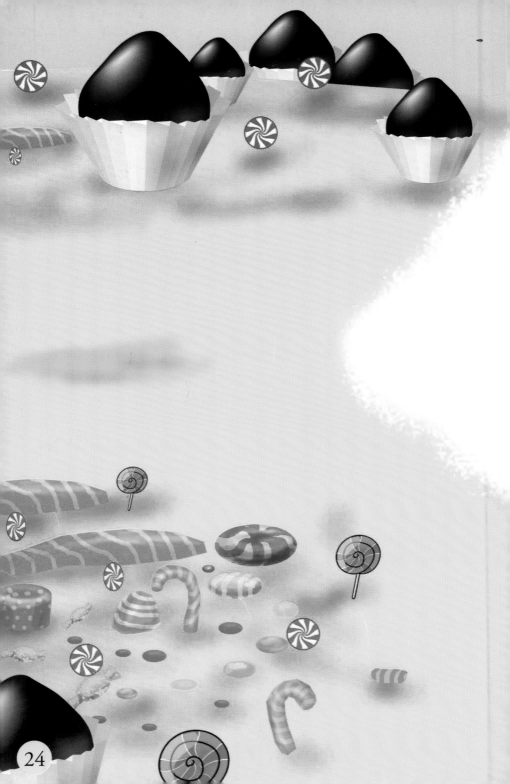

She flies to the Moon.
It has colourful candy parks.

Tina eats some of
the candies.
She takes some for
her friends.

Tina wakes up the next morning.

"Good morning!"
says Mamma.
"Look, Mamma! A coin!"
says Tina.

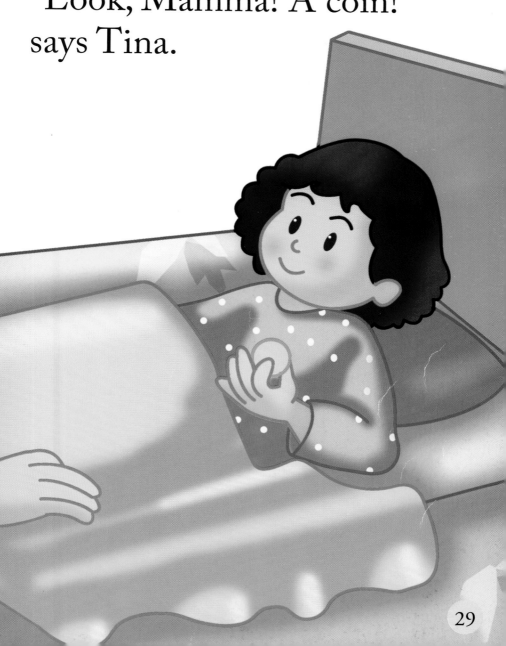

"What will you do with it?"
asks Mamma.

Tina uses it to buy
a bone for Choco!

Know your words

Park - Garden.

Shiny - Clean and bright.

Shakes - Moves something around up and down or from side to side quickly.

Rattles - Makes quick, sharp, knocking sounds.

Draws - Creates a picture, usually with a pencil on a paper.

Jug - A container with a handle, used to hold and pour liquids.

Sinks - Drops downwards, mainly in a liquid.

Slide - Moves smoothly along a surface.

Dreams - A series of thoughts or images crossing your mind as you sleep.

Candy - A type of sweet.